W9-DHM-422

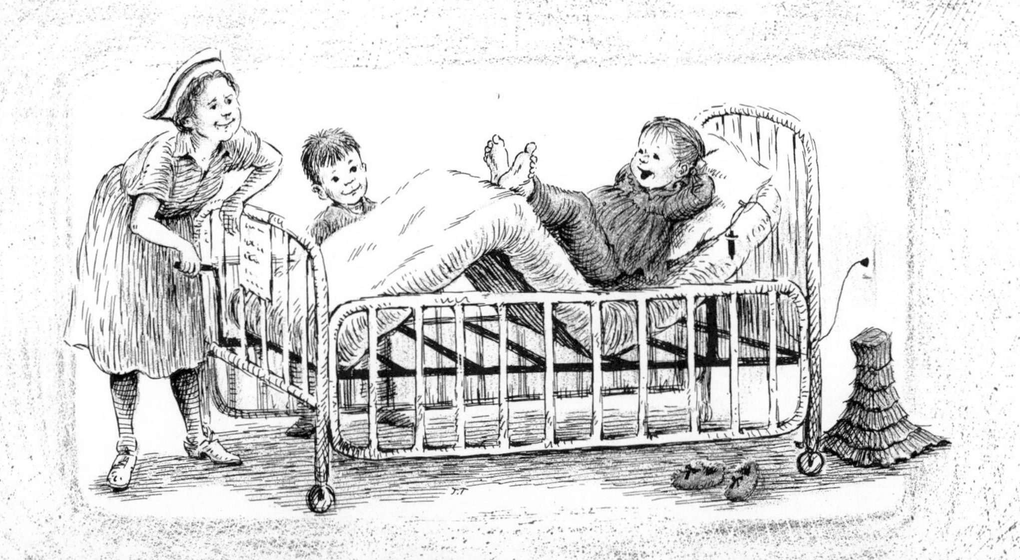

# I THINK I WILL

## GO TO THE HOSPITAL

# I THINK I WILL GO TO THE HOSPITAL

by Jean Tamburine

ABINGDON PRESS
*NASHVILLE* *NEW YORK*

Lithographed in the United States of America

Library of Congress Catalog Card Number: 65-14093

To Boys and Girls Everywhere
and to my
Mother and Father
Helen and Paul Tamburine

# I THINK I WILL

"I will NOT go!" shouted Susy. "I am just not ready."

"Susy, Susy!" said her Mother, "Dr. Dick thinks it is best for you to go to the hospital and have your tonsils removed."

"I don't want to go," Susy shouted again.

"You know how bad you feel when your throat is sore," said Mother. "Remember how many times you can't go out to play?"

"My throat doesn't hurt now," said Susy.

"I know," said Mother, "but we want to keep you well all the time. We'll visit the hospital first. It's a very nice place."

"I don't even want to visit," said Susy. "I'd rather have a sore throat."

She ran to her special place under the chinaberry tree. The duck and the hen and the cat were waiting for her.

"I'm not ready to have my tonsils out," Susy cried.

"Quack!" said her duck.

"Cluck, cluck!" said the hen.

"Meow, meow, meow!" said the cat.

"Do you know why I don't want to go to the hospital?" Susy asked.

The duck and the hen and the cat just sat and looked at poor Susy.

"I don't really know what a hospital is," Susy said.

"Quack," said the duck.
"Cluck, cluck," said the hen.
"Meow, meow, meow," said the cat.
"I won't go," said Susy. "Let's hide."

Susy got behind the stone wall. The duck and the hen and the cat followed her.

"Keep down and don't make any noise," said Susy.

"Susy, Susy!" Mother called. "Come get dressed to go visiting."

Susy kept very quiet. She made herself as small as she could.

"Susy!" Mother called again. "Where are you?"

Susy didn't make a sound. But the duck popped his head over the stone wall.

"Quack!" said the duck.

The hen jumped upon the duck's back.

"Cluck, cluck!" said the hen.

And the cat jumped upon the wall.

"Meow, meow, meow!" cried the cat.

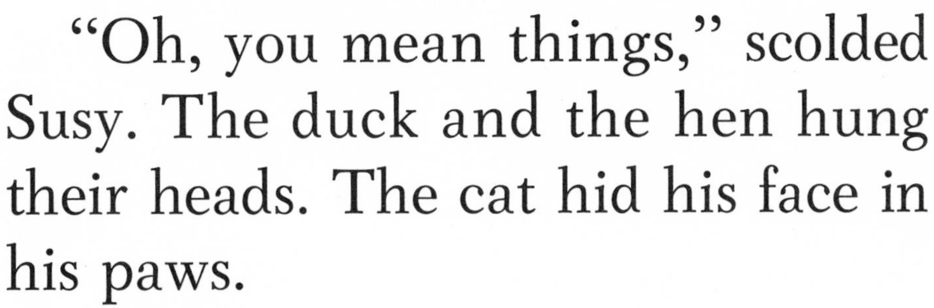

"Oh, you mean things," scolded Susy. The duck and the hen hung their heads. The cat hid his face in his paws.

"Come on in," said Mother.

"I don't want to go," shouted Susy.

"Really, Susy," said Mother, "I do wish you felt better. I have to deliver three presents."

"Presents?" asked Susy. "Who has a birthday?"

"Nobody is having a birthday," said Mother. "I must deliver two get-well presents. The third present is for a new baby."

Susy helped Mother choose her dress and socks. She washed quickly and soon was ready to go. While Susy held the packages Mother drove to Mr. Mullins' house.

"We brought you a present," said Susy. "A get-well present."

"Oh, I like presents," said Mr. Mullins.

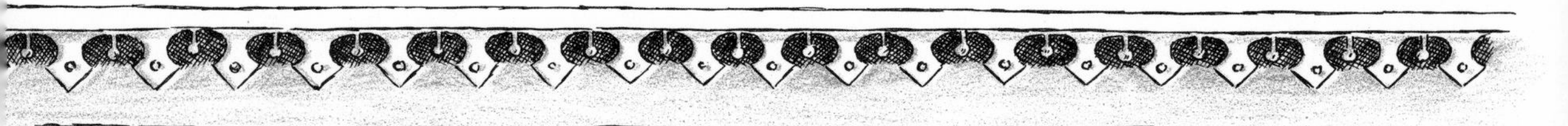

"Open it," said Susy. "It's jam for your toast. Strawberry jam."

"I hope you're feeling better, Mr. Mullins," said Susy's Mother.

"Every day I feel better," said Mr. Mullins. "They took good care of me at the hospital."

Susy and her Mother said good-bye and drove to Jamie's house.

"There's Jamie," Susy said to her Mother, "and he's walking with crutches."

"He has a broken leg," said Mother. "Look at the pictures on his cast."

"Hello, Jamie," said Susy. "We've brought you a get-well present."

Jamie opened his present. It was a book about horses.

"Thank you," he said. "In a little while my leg will be well enough for me to ride a horse."

Susy looked at the pictures on Jamie's cast. She saw a cowboy, a silly rabbit, an airplane, and a clown.

"The doctors and nurses at the hospital drew them," explained Jamie.

"If I went to the hospital to have my tonsils out could I get a cast with pictures?" asked Susy.

"No," laughed Jamie. "Casts are put on broken arms and legs. After the doctor set my leg, the hurt wasn't so bad. Then I liked the hospital."

"It's time to go, Susy," said Mother.

"Where are we going?" asked Susy.

"I am going to see the new baby. You will stay in the waiting room."

"In the hospital?" asked Susy. "Will I be by myself in the waiting room?"

"No. Other people will be waiting too."

The hospital was a very big place. Susy's Mother opened one of the big front doors. Susy looked

around the room. It was big. There were many chairs and many people waiting. Some had flowers. Some had packages wrapped in pretty paper and ribbons.

A man who sat next to Susy had a toy duck.

"I have a REAL duck," said Susy.

"This is for my little boy," said the man.

"Is he very sick?" asked Susy.

"Not really. He had his tonsils out," said the man.

"Oh," said Susy. "Did it hurt?"

"He will have a sore throat for a few days," said the man, "but he won't have so many colds or a sore throat so often."

"Did he get some presents?" asked Susy.

"I don't think so," said the man, "but he doesn't care about that. He wants a ride in a wheelchair."

"I might have my tonsils out," said Susy, "but I'm not ready."

"If the doctor says you should," the man said, "it's a good idea to do what he says."

"Hospitals smell different," said Susy.

"Yes," said the man. "They have a nice, clean odor."

A nurse stopped and said, "Hello! You're Susy, aren't you?"

"Yes," whispered Susy.

"I saw your Mother upstairs," the nurse said. "I took care of you when you were a baby."

"I was in the hospital before?" asked Susy.

"Yes," said the nurse, "you were born here."

"I might have my tonsils out," said Susy.

"Well, this is the place to come," said the nurse. "We will take good care of you."

"I don't want to stay by myself," said Susy.

"You really aren't by yourself. Many boys and girls stay in the hospital."

"Do they get wheelchair rides?" asked Susy.

"Oh, yes," said the nurse. "If they're very good sometimes they get two rides."

"What will they do to me in the hospital?" asked Susy.

"The doctors make you well," said the nurse. "For you, they would take out your tonsils while you are asleep."

"Won't it hurt?" asked Susy.

"Well, you won't know about it when it's happening. Later you will have a sore throat for a few days, and you may not want to eat anything except soft foods—maybe ice cream or soup."

"What else do the doctors do?" asked Susy.

"Sometimes they look inside your mouth with a flashlight. Sometimes an X-ray camera takes a picture of you so the doctor can see inside your body," said the nurse. "Sometimes they make a test to find out about your blood. They use a special needle. The doctor knows how to do this so that it doesn't hurt much."

"What do you do?" asked Susy.

"A nurse takes your temperature with a thermometer to see how hot your body is. And if you need medicine, a nurse gives it to you. If you are supposed to stay in bed, your food is brought to you on a tray."

Susy thought about these things.

"Your Mother and Father and your Grandparents can visit you," said the nurse.

"I would like get-well presents and a wheelchair ride, but I don't like to hurt," said Susy.

"No one likes to hurt," said the nurse. "But most hurts don't last long."

"Sometimes I want my Mother and Daddy at night," said Susy.

"There's a little buzzer beside your bed," said the nurse. "You just push the button when you need something. A nurse comes."

"Could I bring my doll?" asked Susy. "And a book?"

"Of course," said the nurse.

Susy looked up. Her Mother had come back.

"I hope to see you soon, Susy," said the nurse.

Susy just smiled.

As soon as Susy and her Mother got home, Susy ran to the backyard.

"All of you are sick," Susy said to her duck and her hen and her cat. "I am the nurse." She bandaged the duck's head.

"Open your mouth!" Susy said to the hen. "Let me see your tonsils." And she shone a flashlight in the hen's mouth.

"Cat," said Susy, "I will put casts on your legs." She bandaged the cat's legs and drew pictures on the bandages. The cat didn't like this very much. 

"You know something?" asked Susy. "I am going to the hospital to have my tonsils out, and then we will really know how to play hospital." She ran to her Mother.

"When can I go to the hospital?" she asked.

"Dr. Dick says you may go tomorrow," said Mother.

There was a terrible noise from the backyard.

The duck and the hen and the cat were tired of their bandages. The duck tried to knock his bandages off. The hen ran in circles. The cat howled because he couldn't get his bandages off. They quacked and clucked and howled loudly.

"Oh," cried Susy. "I forgot to leave a buzzer for you." And she ran to take off the bandages.

The next day Susy and Mother packed her suitcase. They packed pajamas, slippers, a bathrobe, toothbrush and toothpaste, and a hairbrush. Susy chose a doll and a book.

Her Mother and Father took her to the hospital. As they walked in the big front door, Susy saw Stevie, her friend from school.

"I've had my tonsils taken out," said Stevie with a big, big grin.

"You have?" asked Susy.

"And I got to ride down to the operating room on a table!" said Stevie. "It has wheels! The doctor told me to take a deep breath. The stuff I smelled made me go to sleep. When I waked up the doctor had taken out my tonsils!"

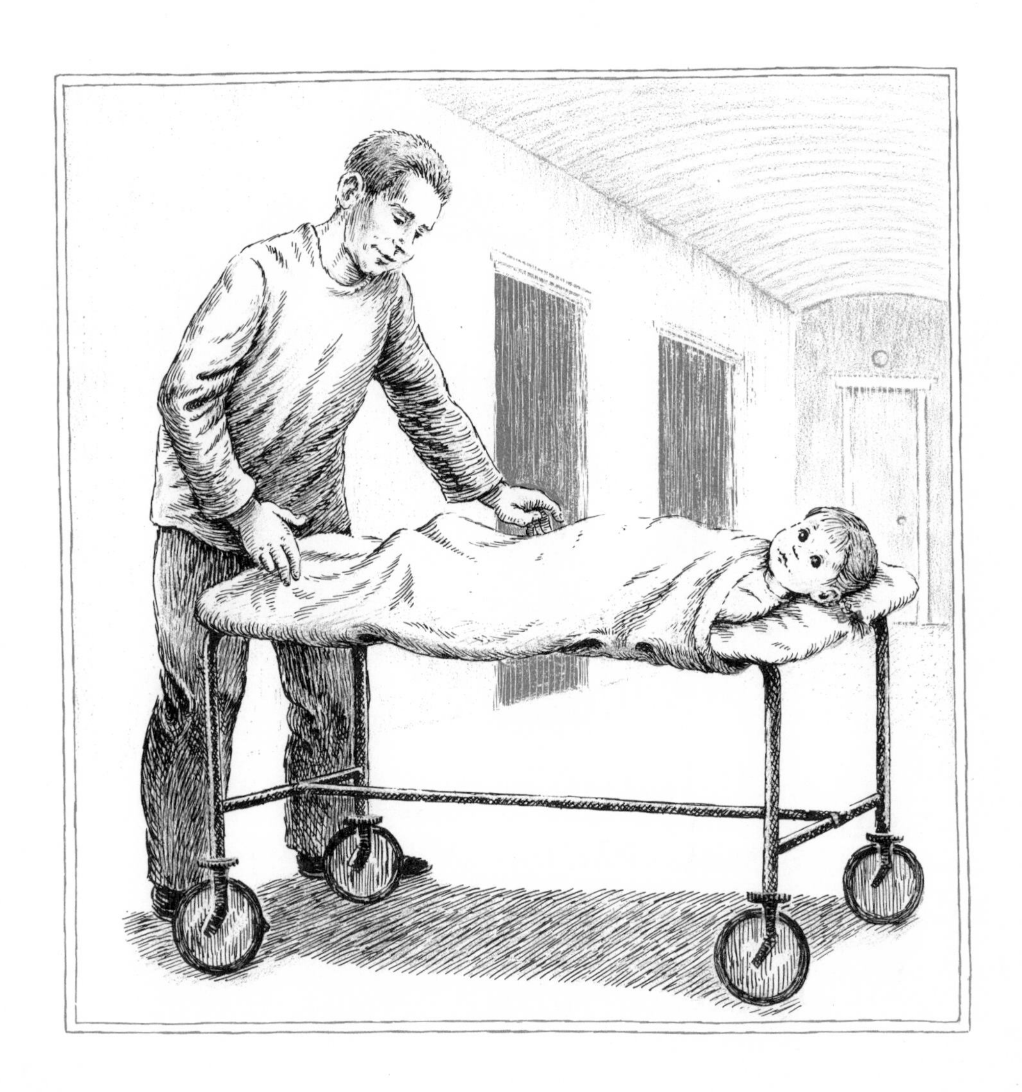

"Did it hurt much?" asked Susy.

"My throat hurt," said Stevie, "but it's all right now. I'm going home."

"Did you get two rides in a wheelchair?" asked Susy.

"Yes," said Stevie.

"Say good-bye to Stevie," Mother said to Susy. "The nurse is here to take you to your room."

Susy and her Mother and Father followed the nurse to the elevator. Up, up, up they went. They got out at the children's floor and went into a big room. There were

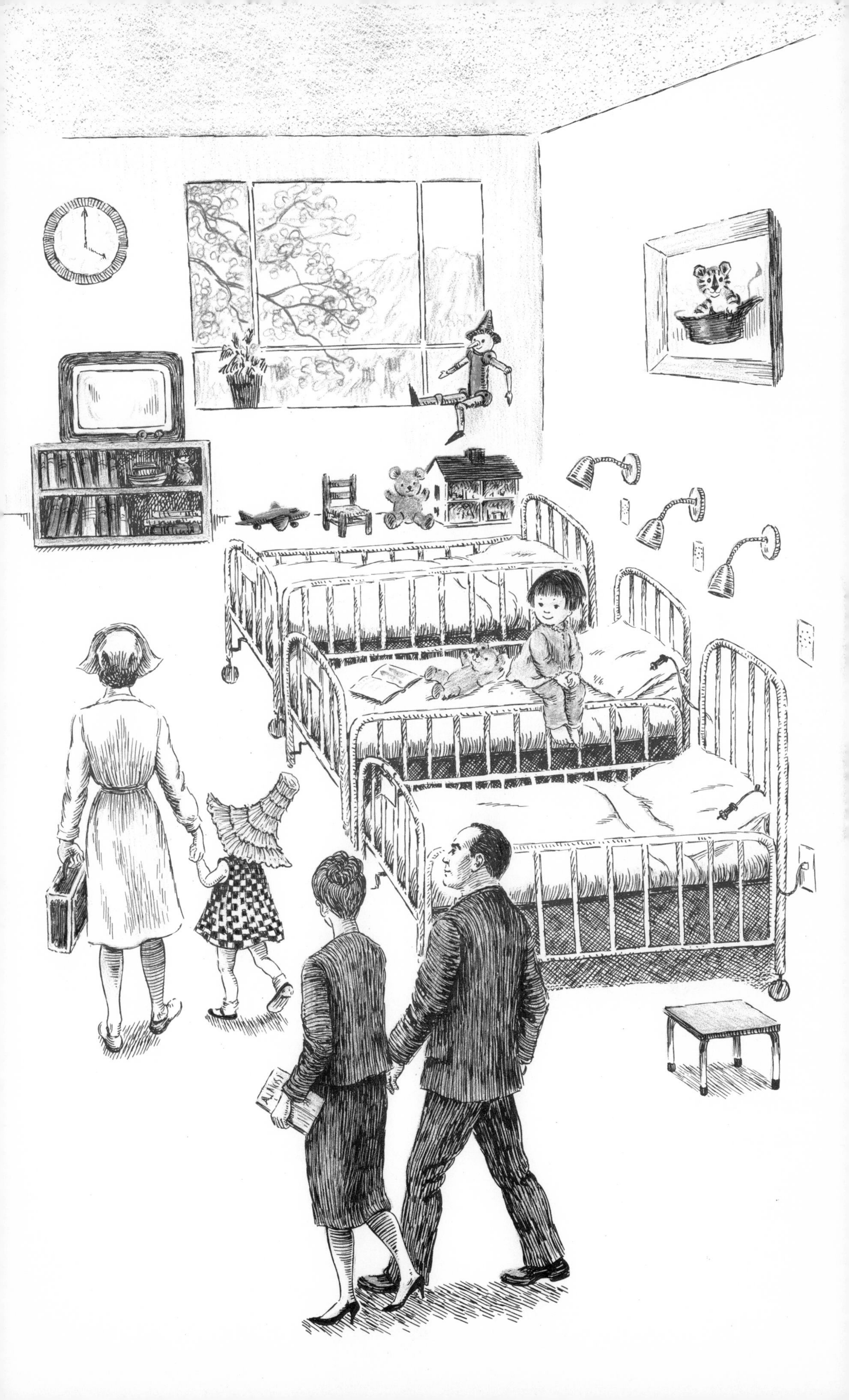

six beds in the room. Some of them already had children in them. A little girl smiled at Susy.

"This bed is for Susy," said the nurse.

"Here's my buzzer," said Susy.

"Yes," said the nurse, "there's your buzzer. Use it only if you really need something."

The nurse looked at her watch. "It's time for your Mother and Father to be going, Susy. Shall I help you change into your pajamas?"

"I can undress myself," said Susy.

Susy's Father winked at her. "We will see you later," he said.

"Good-bye for now," said Mother.

"Good-bye," said Susy as she looked at her bed.

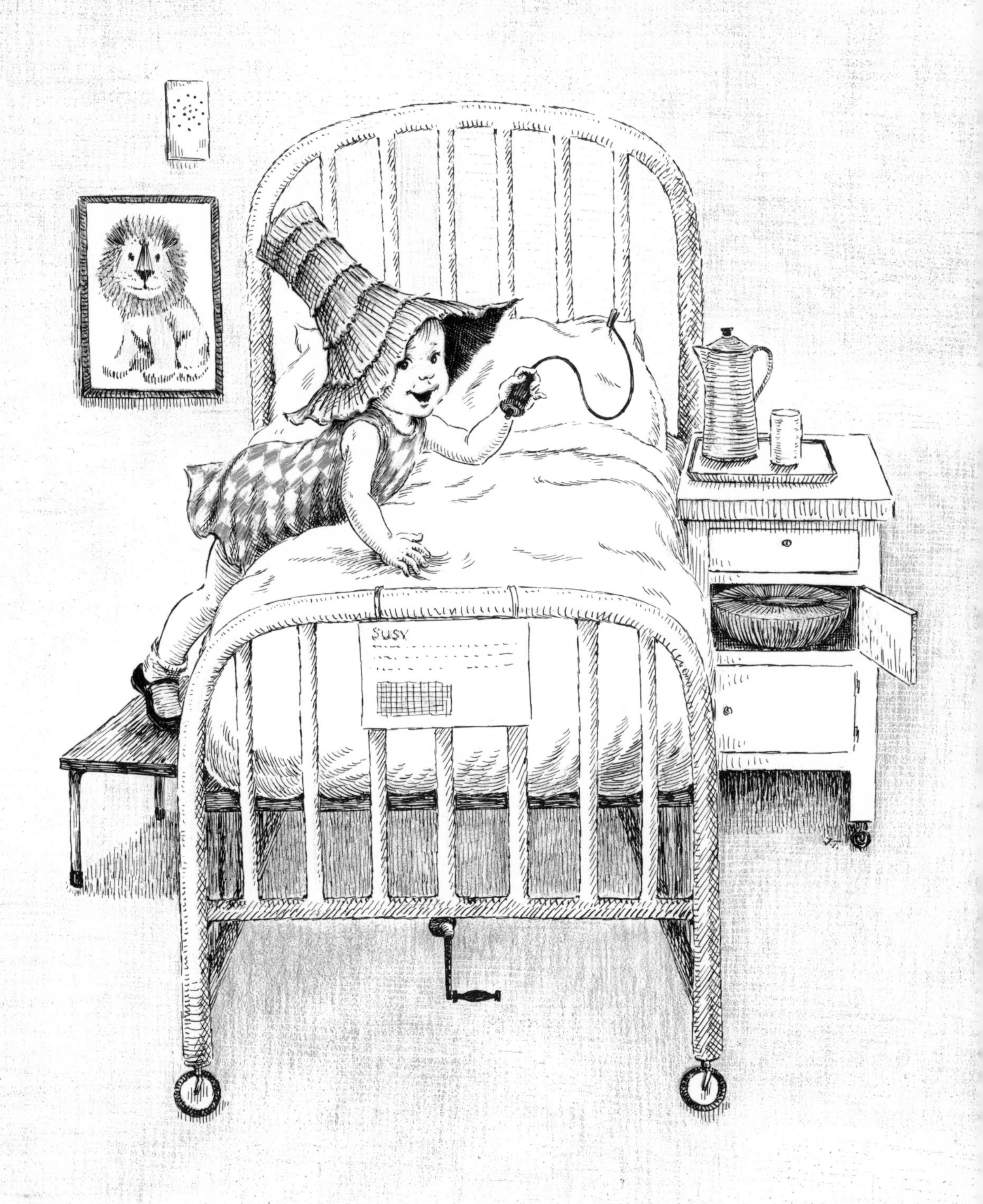


"I'll be right here if you need me," said the nurse. "Just—"

"I know," said Susy, "just press the buzzer!"

Susy's Father laughed. "You are really going to have something to tell to the duck and the hen and the cat. What do you think?"

Susy laughed too. "Oh, yes! I THINK I WILL!"

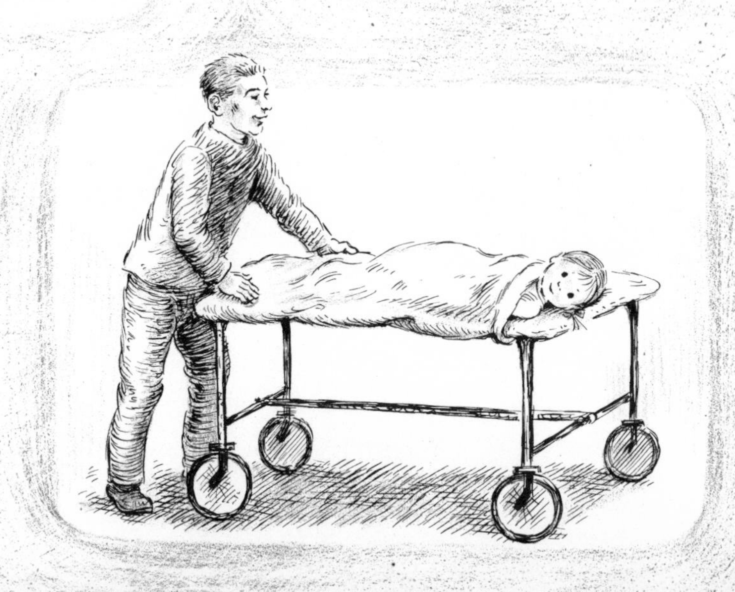